KIDS
T...
OWN ADVENTURE STORIES!

SECRET OF THE DOLPHINS

BY EDWARD PACKARD

ILLUSTRATED BY TOM LA PADULA

BANTAM BOOKS
NEW YORK · TORONTO · LONDON · SYDNEY · AUCKLAND

RL 4, age 10 and up

SECRET OF THE DOLPHINS
A Bantam Book / April 1993

CHOOSE YOUR OWN ADVENTURE® *is a registered trademark of
Bantam Books, a division of Bantam Doubleday Dell Publishing
Group, Inc.
Registered in U.S. Patent and Trademark Office and elsewhere.*

Original conception of Edward Packard

*Cover art by Catherine Huerta
Interior illustrations by Tom La Padula*

ISBN: 0-553-29300-1

Published simultaneously in the United States and Canada

---

*Bantam Books are published by Bantam Books, a division of Bantam
Doubleday Dell Publishing Group, Inc. Its trademark, consisting of the
words "Bantam Books" and the portrayal of a rooster, is Registered in
U.S. Patent and Trademark Office and in other countries. Marca Regis-
trada. Bantam Books, 1540 Broadway, New York, New York 10036.*

PRINTED IN THE UNITED STATES OF AMERICA

OPM   10 9 8 7 6 5 4

SECRET OF
THE DOLPHINS

SECRET OF
THE DOLPHINS

KAUAI   OAHU   MOLOKAI   MAUI

HAWAII

NIIHAU

LANAI

KAHOOLAWE

SUN
LOTION

WARNING!!!

Do not read this book straight through from beginning to end. These pages contain many different adventures that you may have when you spend a summer in Hawaii as an intern at the world-famous Dolphin Institute.

From time to time as you read along, you will be asked to make a choice. After you make your decision, follow the instructions to find out what happens to you next.

To discover the secret of the dolphins, you'll have to outwit a vicious criminal, survive a natural catastrophe, and win the trust of the dolphins themselves. If you're smart and you're brave, you can do it.

Good luck!

You can hardly believe that school let out for the summer only two days ago as you look out the window of the small plane that has carried you to the island of Kauai, in Hawaii. The plane pulls up to the terminal building and stops with a jerk. A minute later the hatch opens, and you climb down the boarding ladder. You sling your duffel bag over your shoulder, then pause for a moment to smell the fresh, fragrant air.

A lean, athletic-looking man with a close-cropped beard strides up to you. "Hi there. Are you going to Luali Cove—the Dolphin Institute?"

"That's right."

He smiles and holds out a hand. "Jack Banta. I'm a graduate student on the staff. I've come to meet you." He grabs your duffel and slings it over his shoulder. "Welcome to Hawaii."

"Thanks," you say, smiling back at Banta. You can tell already that you're going to like him.

You're glad of that, because you'll be spending the next two months at the Dolphin Institute. You were awarded a scholarship for the institute's summer program, and you and two other summer interns will be helping the scientists there in their study of dolphins. The institute is paying your airfare, room and board, plus a small stipend. You don't know yet what projects you'll be working on, but you like dolphins—and even more, you like the idea of spending the summer in Hawaii.

Turn to page 2.

Banta drives you along a winding, mountainous road from which you occasionally get spectacular views of the sea. You lean forward in your seat to take in the lush scenery on both sides of the road. Glancing up, you see a blimp passing overhead. You smile as you read the sign on it: *Don't Miss Maui.*

"It's beautiful here," you say.

"I have no complaints," Banta says, flashing you a smile. "Do you have any questions about the institute?"

"How many people work there?" you ask.

"Well, Dr. Vivaldi's in charge. Besides her, there's just a marine biologist, a zoologist, and myself. Plus visiting scientists who drop in from time to time, and student interns."

"What sort of work have you been doing?"

"The institute was founded six years ago, and most of our work has involved studying dolphin societies. But a year ago we began an intensive study of dolphin communication. We believe that someday humans and dolphins will be able to talk to each other. But there are lots of problems to be solved. In fact, just figuring out what the problems *are* is quite a task." He glances at you. "But I have a feeling we're going to make a breakthrough this summer."

Go on to the next page.

"Sounds as if I got here just in time," you say with a grin. "Are there other scientists studying dolphin communication?"

"There are," Banta says. "Dolphin communication is a pretty hot topic right now. But none of the other teams is as advanced as we are. In fact, we actually have to worry about spies. There are plenty of people who don't have respect for dolphins but want to use them for their own selfish purposes—everything from finding sunken treasure to terrorist activities."

Go on to page 5.

The Jeep passes over the crest of a hill, and there, stretched out before you, are the pale blue waters of Luali Cove. Banta turns onto a winding gravel drive that leads to a comfortable-looking, rustic lodge. About a dozen smaller cabins are scattered alongside the cove. A dock extends out into the water in front of the main lodge. A couple of sea skiffs are tied to the pilings alongside the dock, and a large catamaran is moored two hundred feet offshore.

Banta takes you into the lodge and introduces you to the staff members. Then he shows you around the grounds. "This used to be a resort," he says. "The owner became fascinated by all the dolphins that came into the cove. When he retired, he donated the entire place to the Dolphin Institute. Our director, Dr. Nera Vivaldi, lives in the main lodge. You'll be staying in the lodge, too, along with the other two summer interns, Karen Meyers and Dave Chang. The other staff members and I live in the cabins. But we all work in the main lodge when we're not out on the water, or under it."

Turn to page 56.

6

You catch sight of Dave, by now just a speck on the horizon. It's obvious he didn't hear the siren. You're very worried about him, but right now you've got to think about yourself. Should you head out to sea, try to sail back into the cove, or just beach your board as fast as you can?

The nearest land doesn't look too inviting—just a rocky, ragged coast, thick with tangled vegetation. You might have trouble climbing to safety. Maybe it would be better to try to make it back into the cove. The wind is more favorable to you coming from this angle. You're pretty sure you can stay upright on your board and sail through the inlet. On the other hand, if you head out after Dave into the open sea, you may be able to ride out the tidal wave.

If you try to make it into the cove,
turn to page 58.

If you land immediately, turn to page 27.

If you head out to sea, turn to page 68.

You wince when you hear this. Dr. Vivaldi is a brilliant scientist, but that doesn't mean she's wise to the ways of men like Mr. X. She's so used to being outspoken and forthright that she couldn't see that this was one time a lie would have been justified.

A smile forms on Mr. X's face. "So, since you like dolphins so much, we'll let you swim with them." He stalks out the door, muttering something to the gunman as he exits. The gunman then marches the three of you up on deck and makes you line up by the rail. He stands a few paces away, his weapon at the ready.

"What do you think they're going to do to us?" you whisper.

"These men are pirates—criminals of the sea," Dr. Vivaldi says in a tone of disgust. "I wouldn't be surprised if they made us walk the plank."

Nearby, two men are lowering a small boat over the side of the yacht.

"What's the boat for?" you ask the gunman.

"It's for you," he says. "We don't want you drowning near where we're diving."

A sailor lowers a ladder. The boat, a dory with an outboard motor, splashes gently in the water. Another sailor jumps in, starts the engine, and brings the boat under the ladder.

The gunman gestures with his weapon. "Okay, down the ladder and into the boat."

Turn to page 35.

8

You follow the dolphin, wading through the pools of water amid the rocks. Then you stop short as you spot a baby dolphin swimming frantically back and forth in one of the tiny shallow pools. It must have washed in from the ocean and gotten trapped when the wave receded. The larger dolphin must be its mother. She wants you to help her baby!

You wade in. The baby dolphin thrashes wildly, more frightened than ever. You're afraid it will bite you, but you've got to help it. The tide would never come high enough to free it.

You kneel down in the water and cradle the dolphin in your arms. Surprisingly it doesn't struggle. Perhaps it understands that you're trying to help. With a great effort you lift it, wade out of the pool, and clamber up on the coral shelf that lies between you and the sea. The creature in your arms is only a baby, but it must weigh almost a hundred pounds. You grit your teeth, trying to keep your footing on the wet coral. You reach the edge of the shelf. A wave splashes around your knees. Your strength is gone, and you start to lose your balance. The dolphin scoots out of your arms and splashes into the surf. It swims toward its waiting mother, and you fall, exhausted, into an oncoming wave.

You're too tired to do anything but lie in the waves sloshing in on the shore. You close your eyes and float, wondering if you'll ever get home again.

Turn to page 16.

10

A scream comes up out of the water, not from a dolphin but from the first gunman, who was swimming back to the yacht. He sinks beneath the waves.

Dr. Vivaldi starts toward Mr. X, but he whirls around and points the pistol at her. She stops in her tracks. "Don't make a move, any of you," he snarls.

"Can't you see that you should leave the dolphins alone?" Dr. Vivaldi says. "You'll only bring misery upon yourself if you don't stop what you're doing."

"You're telling me to stop?" Mr. X exclaims incredulously. "Because a few animals are in my way? Ha!"

You and your friends try to argue with him, but he marches you back to the forward stateroom and locks you in.

"Well," Grace says, once you're alone, "the dolphins are proving to be even more amazing than we suspected."

"Maybe they can save us," you say.

Dr. Vivaldi shakes her head. "I'm afraid that's wishful thinking. The dolphins had the advantage of surprise just now, but they're really no match for Mr. X and his arsenal."

Turn to page 20.

When you report to Banta and Dr. Vivaldi what happened, they are very excited.

"This is one more piece of proof that dolphins have advanced intelligence," you say.

"I feel awed by these animals," Banta says. "They have neither hands nor feet, nor can they come out of the sea, nor can they speak the way we do. Yet they are as special in their own way as we humans are in ours."

"I feel that way, too, more so with each new discovery," Dr. Vivaldi says. "Let's all redouble our efforts to uncover the secrets of the dolphins. In the process I predict we'll learn a great deal about ourselves."

The End

12

Banta seems hypnotized by the tapes, but you're beginning to wish you'd gone windsurfing with the others. You're not being any help to Banta sitting here, and it doesn't seem as if he's going to be making any breakthroughs today after all.

Finally the tape ends, the room is silent again, and the printer stops spewing out paper. Banta enters some commands into the computer. Then he turns around and notices you sitting there. He starts, and you realize that he must have forgotten you were in the room.

"Oh, sorry, I don't think I'm explaining enough," he says. "The sounds you just heard were a conversation between Alceste and Hermione. The computer may tell us more in a few minutes, but I think that they were talking about a school of fish they'd found."

"Really? You can tell that?"

"Yes, but that alone is not a big achievement. Just because a dolphin makes a sound that means 'fish over that way' doesn't mean they'll be able to talk with us."

"Then why did you think you were on the brink of a discovery?"

"I'll show you," Banta says. He inserts a different tape into the machine and switches it on. Dolphin sounds fill the room. The monitor and the printer start up again.

Turn to page 66.

"We can't be sure," Banta says. "But it's significant that the first tape was made when the dolphins knew we were around, while the second was made late at night with a secretly hidden microphone."

"You mean they say things when they think they're alone that they don't when humans are around?"

Banta grins. "That's *exactly* what I mean."

At that moment Dr. Vivaldi comes in. "There you are," she says to you. "I was going to take the interns on a drive around the island. I hear Karen and Dave went windsurfing, but maybe you'd like to come with me. It will give you a chance to see some of the great scenery we have around here."

You glance at Banta.

"Go ahead," he says. "We can't do anything more until I get my analysis back from the supercomputer. I should have it by late this evening." He then explains to Dr. Vivaldi what he's discovered.

"Jack, this is very exciting," she says. "Let's discuss it tomorrow at breakfast. For now, why don't you take a couple of hours off and come along on our drive?"

"Sounds great," he replies. "Let's go."

Turn to page 37.

You turn and start swimming again. But by now, you're even less certain that you're going in the right direction.

By the time dawn breaks, you're too tired and chilled to swim anymore. And when you see a large fin breaking the water, coming toward you, it's not the fin of a dolphin.

The End

16

You feel something nudging you. Looking up, you see that it's the mother dolphin. You wonder what she's doing—maybe she wants to thank you. But then she noses under your body and lifts you up. You slide onto her back and grab her dorsal fin to keep from falling off. Suddenly she's swimming, carrying you out to sea. She speeds up but keeps to the surface so you're able to breathe.

You look over and see the baby dolphin swimming alongside. It seems to have forgotten its ordeal as it frolics and plays in the water. At first you're worried, wondering where the dolphin is taking you. But then your heart leaps for joy— you're heading straight for Luali cove!

You manage to hang on while the dolphin cruises through the inlet and, to your astonishment, takes you right up to the shore in front of the Dolphin Institute! The dock and small boats have been washed away by the tidal wave, but the main lodge hardly looks damaged at all.

Turn to page 78.

"Was that all they said?" you ask.

"No, they talked about a lot of other things," Banta says. "But even the supercomputer couldn't decipher most of it. Of course, the more recordings it listens to, the more data it will compile. Eventually we should be able to understand most of what they say."

"This is extraordinary," Dr. Vivaldi says. "But what fascinates me most is that the dolphins seem to have been talking about things they would never discuss when humans were around."

"Do you really think it's fair to spy on them?" Karen asks.

"I've thought about that," Banta says. "If I were caught spying on humans this way, I'd be pretty embarrassed. Why should I not pay the same respect to these creatures, who may be just as intelligent and aware as we are?"

"It's in the interests of science," Dave says.

"A lot of bad things have been done in the 'interests of science,' " you point out.

"But we aren't going to harm the dolphins—if anything, we want to help them," Dave says.

"That's true," says Dr. Vivaldi. "So I think I'll approve Jack's snooping. But we must remember that although we wouldn't use what we learn to hurt the dolphins, there are others who might. For that reason we must keep everything we find secret until we're sure that no harm can come from revealing it."

Turn to page 100.

A few seconds later, a tremendous jolt sends the bow high in the air. The gunman flies over the rail and into the ocean. Water pours into the stern of the boat. The sailor at the wheel shouts in surprise and grabs hold of the ladder. Dr. Vivaldi and Grace cling to the thwarts. You leap to the controls and rev the throttle, hoping to escape before your kidnappers can recover their wits. But the engine stalls, and a second later another gunman has a weapon trained on you. "Climb up the ladder," he yells.

The three of you have no choice but to obey. As soon as you climb back aboard the yacht, a sailor scrambles past you and drops down, expecting to land in the boat. But at the last minute the boat is jerked aside, and the sailor lands in the water. He grabs for the boat, but it's already out of his reach, moving away from the yacht. The dolphins are towing it!

Mr. X has rushed out onto the deck to see what the commotion is about. He whips out his pistol and fires, trying to hit a dolphin.

Turn to page 10.

20

Night comes, with no further sign of your captors. The three of you try to get some sleep, but of course that's not easy. The events of the day keep racing through your head. You wonder what the morning will bring.

Will there be war—humans vs. dolphins? It's horrible to contemplate. The dolphins have always had a reputation for gentleness. But their special playground has been invaded, and they certainly have the right to try to drive the invaders off. Still thinking these disturbing thoughts, you finally drift off to sleep.

You're awakened in the night by a curious noise, a thumping in the bow of the boat, as if a wave had thrown something heavy against the hull. You test the door to the stateroom. It's still locked.

You wonder what's going on, and if the dolphins are involved somehow. For a moment, it feels as though the yacht may be moving. But then you decide you must be imagining things. It's a calm night and the boat is securely anchored. After a while you go back to sleep.

Turn to page 88.

Dr. Vivaldi gets up from the table. "I'm going to go call Grace right now. The moon is almost full—if the weather holds, we could track Alceste even at night." She turns to Frank. "Take the Jeep out to the point and see if you can spot Alceste going through the inlet. Bring your radiophone so you can let us know where he heads once he's out in the ocean."

"You bet." Frank hurries out. Dr. Vivaldi follows him. A few minutes later she returns.

"Grace loved the idea. Not only is she willing to lend us the blimp, she'll even come along to pilot it. Now, we have no time to waste. I'd like an intern to come with me on the blimp." She lays a hand on your shoulder. "You've shown the most initiative by working in the lab with Jack Banta, so I'm giving you first choice. You can leave with me in five minutes for the airport, or stay here and work on the computers."

"I'd like to come along," you say immediately.

"Are you sure? I'd better warn you, the blimp trip will probably be quite tedious," she says. "You won't be able to go swimming or sailing for quite a while, and tracking Alceste will mean staring down at the ocean through binoculars, hour after hour. The biggest discovery might come right here in the computer lab. So think carefully before you make up your mind."

---

*If you decide to go on the blimp,
turn to page 76.*

*If you decide to stay at the cove,
turn to page 108.*

"Harry is one of the top divers around here," Cap'n Bob says, gesturing toward the other man, who nods at you. Harry is small but muscular, with the leathery skin of someone who's spent a life at sea. You hold out your hand. He shakes it so hard it hurts.

Harry casts off the lines. Cap'n Bob coaxes the boat out into the channel, then guns the engine. A few minutes later the boat passes through the inlet, rolling and pitching as it ploughs into the ocean swells.

You give Cap'n Bob the latitude and longitude of the dolphin city and follow him to the worktable, where he marks the spot on the chart. "Interesting," he says, pointing. "It says here that there are breakers right there. That's usually a sign of dangerous shoals. There's so little water over them that when a bit of sea is running, the waves break just as if they were coming up on the beach. Ships and boats stay clear of places like that." He looks at you suspiciously.

"That's probably why the city hasn't been discovered," you say.

Cap'n Bob grunts. "Maybe so." He measures the distance on the chart. "We should be there before sundown," he says. "We'll drop a marker buoy and then just lay off overnight, taking turns on watch. We'll start diving at dawn. If there's treasure down there, we'll find it."

Turn to page 80.

Ten minutes later you're airborne in the blimp, cruising over the ocean. Grace estimates that you'll catch up with Alceste in a little over half an hour.

You scan the surface of the waves through your binoculars. The ocean is quite calm, with only occasional whitecaps on the crests of the swells. But after half an hour has passed, you still see no sign of the dolphin.

Dr. Vivaldi glances at her watch. "It's still a little too soon," she says. "Give it another five minutes or so."

"I hope Alceste doesn't change course," you say.

Dr. Vivaldi shows you the chart she is holding. She runs her finger along the north coast of Kauai. "I don't think he'll change course until he rounds this point," she says. She picks up her binoculars. "We'll both keep watch until we spot him."

Fifteen more minutes pass, then twenty. Dr. Vivaldi begins to look worried. She asks Grace to slow down and steer the blimp in a circle.

"Maybe Alceste decided to take some time out to chase a few fish," you say.

Dr. Vivaldi nods. "You're probably right."

Turn to page 48.

That night you meet the other interns, Karen and Dave, who are both about your age. Karen is from Iowa, and she's never seen the ocean before, much less a dolphin. Dave is from Los Angeles. He plans to be a marine biologist someday, and he's been on a couple of whale watch trips, where he saw dolphins swim alongside his ship. "I'm more interested in dolphins than whales because they're closer to human size," he says. "I feel we can really get to know them."

You also meet Dr. Nera Vivaldi, the director of the institute. She's a small, gray-haired woman who must be well up in her sixties, but she looks as trim and fit as an athlete.

There's a pool table in the lodge, and after dinner you start a game with Karen and Dave. Dr. Vivaldi joins you for your second game. "You three picked a good summer to be here," she tells you. "We're on the edge of a breakthrough in dolphin communication, and you're likely to be here when it happens."

Turn to page 63.

You look at the dock and immediately see what he means. There are only a few inches of water at the end of it, and all along the shore you can see exposed rocks and coral reefs that were covered before.

"Let's go a little higher," Karen says. "Just to be sure."

The three of you scramble up through the thick ground cover, trying to get as high as you can before the tsunami strikes. You keep moving until you reach the top of a high, flat-topped boulder. Then you turn around and watch the ocean again, squinting to try to catch a glimpse of Frank or Dave.

"What do you think will happen to those guys out on the ocean?" Karen asks, looking worried.

"Strange thing," Pierre says. "They may be okay out there. They can just rise and fall, as if they were riding a roller coaster. Along the shore is really the most dangerous place to be."

Turn to page 104.

You're not going to take a chance on trying to make it through the inlet and into the cove before the wave hits. Instead, you race to the nearest land. You beach your board on a coral shelf awash in surf. Beyond it are pools of water surrounded by sharp rocks, and further back, the steep bank thick with jungle growth.

You wade through a shallow pool and scramble up on the land at the foot of the bank. When you stop to look back you're shocked to see that the water is receding, as if the tide were suddenly going out. You think you know what that means, and in a moment your suspicions are confirmed. On the horizon you see a wall of water moving toward you—the tsunami!

You grapple with the tangled vines and bushes, struggling to get up the bank. The wave is getting closer—you've got to get higher before it breaks. You grab a vine and heave yourself up, then scramble over a bluff and claw your way through the brush.

With a thunderous roar, the wave breaks and surges up the slope. You lock your arms around a tree. The water hits you like a dozen fire hoses, whirling you around, pelting your body with sticks, stones, roots, branches, and other loose objects.

You never let go of the tree. The water swirls around your chest for a few moments, then recedes. You relax your grip and collapse on the wet, salty ground.

Turn to page 62.

28

Nikko is more than willing to go along with the plan, and the next morning you set out with him at 6:00 A.M., bound for the fishing grounds off the point.

Everything goes smoothly as you motor out of the cove and through the inlet. Nikko helps you bait the line with the microphone on it, scenting it with iodine so fish won't strike at it. Once you're outside the inlet, Nikko drops the line overboard.

You listen eagerly to the first dolphin sounds. Some of them are new to you. One of them seems very much like the sound that means, "I'm angry"—the same one you heard yesterday. Then, without warning, the line goes dead.

You look through the door to the cabin. Nikko is pulling up the line. The end has been cut off—bitten clean through. The bait and the microphone are gone.

You watch the frayed string coming aboard. "I guess a fish got it," you say.

"Not possible," Nikko says. "It wasn't cut anywhere near the bait. That line was cut on purpose. And I bet one of your dolphins did it."

Somehow the dolphins must have known about your plan. Maybe they heard you and Nikko talking right through the hull of the boat. Maybe they saw you climb aboard. In any event, you figure you've got absolute proof now how intelligent these animals are.

Turn to page 11.

"We're studying dolphins," you say, "and we ask that you stay well clear."

"Will do," the answer comes back.

The yacht alters course and heads off at an angle.

Dr. Vivaldi is still leaning over the computer, absorbed with the sounds coming from the hydrophone. Finally she takes off her earphones and grins at you.

"The dolphins are having a great time down there. I can't understand what they're saying, but they're making the kinds of sounds we hear when they're playing and having lots of fun."

"When will we have a sound picture of the ocean floor?" you ask.

Dr. Vivaldi glances down at the computer. "It's being processed now. We'll get a crude picture—an echograph—in a couple of minutes. When we get back we'll run our tapes through the supercomputer. It will be able to enhance the echograph a lot more, and maybe even tell us what the dolphins are talking about."

While the two of you are waiting for the echograph, you tell Dr. Vivaldi about your conversation with the captain of the *Sea Fox*.

She scans the horizon with her binoculars. "I see the yacht. It's lying off at a distance. I bet they'll come back to this spot as soon as we leave."

"What can we do about it?"

"Not much. We're on the high seas. They have as much right to be here as we do."

Turn to page 53.

An hour and a half later, the Coast Guard calls to say that they've picked up Dave and Frank drifting in the ocean. They were both thrown from their crafts, but they rode the waves up and down and didn't get a scratch. They couldn't make it to shore, however. The current was taking them out to sea when a helicopter pilot spotted them. They are shaken up and dehydrated and are staying in the hospital overnight.

You're relieved that Frank and Dave are okay. Unfortunately, however, the damage to the Dolphin Institute's cabins, dock, and boats is considerable. Dr. Vivaldi tells you that the place will have to close for repairs for the rest of the summer. So the next day you pack up, bid your new friends good-bye, and head home.

As you say good-bye to Dr. Vivaldi, she shakes your hand warmly. "We had a bad break," she says, "but at least everyone's alive and well. I hope you can come back next summer."

"Maybe," you say, but you're thinking that next summer you might want to go somewhere a good long way from the ocean.

The End

You swim under the air bag until you feel as if your lungs are going to burst. Then suddenly you're out, taking great gulps of air. You can see the yacht, almost out of sight in the distance. You turn and look back toward the air bag. It's still sinking quickly. In a moment the last of it vanishes beneath the waves.

Alone now, you look up in the sky, hoping to see a rescue plane. The Coast Guard must have gotten Grace's Mayday signal. If not, then you're in big trouble. The water is warm, and you're a good swimmer, but it will be dark soon, and there are no planes or ships in sight. You tread water, trying not to panic.

Then, about half a mile away, you see something breaking the surface of the water. It's a dolphin! Soon you see several more, their tails flipping up as they dive.

Your first impulse is to swim toward the dolphins. Maybe, somehow, they can help you—your chances of being rescued seem pretty slim. Still, Grace did give the blimp's position before it went down. If a rescue party is looking for you, it's a lot more likely to find you if you stay put.

If you just float in the same spot, turn to page 38.

If you swim toward the dolphins, turn to page 96.

34

You and Dr. Vivaldi unstrap yourselves, grab your life preservers, and fight your way through the inrushing water. You swing open the hatch and dive through it, with Dr. Vivaldi and Grace right behind you. The three of you swim away from the wreck, which is sinking rapidly.

You tread water and look around. The yacht is heading toward you at top speed. It must be coming to pick you all up. You don't know what its passengers want with you—and you're not sure you want to stick around to find out.

The blimp's cabin is now completely underwater. Patches of the huge deflated air bag are still floating, held up by air bubbles. You realize that if you were to dive under the air bag and come up in one of the bubbles, the people on the yacht would probably think you'd drowned. But then what? You're at least fifty miles from shore —there's no way you could make it back on your own.

*If you hide under the air bag,
turn to page 91.*

*If you tread water and wait for the yacht
to pick you up, turn to page 98.*

You start down the ladder, with Grace and Dr. Vivaldi right behind you. As you step into the boat, a dolphin appears about twenty yards away. Its head stays above the surface for a long time, an inquiring eye fixed upon you. You wonder if it somehow knows what's happening.

The gunman is the last one to get in the boat. He stands up in the bow where he can cover you with his weapon. The sailor at the wheel revs the engine. Someone on the yacht casts off the line, and the small boat slowly begins to pull away.

Turn to page 19.

At breakfast the next morning, Banta tells everyone what he learned the night before. "The supercomputer can analyze far more possibilities than our equipment can," Banta explains to you, Karen, and Dave. "As a result, it can begin to interpret some of the dolphins' language, which of course is nothing like our own. For the dolphins two different sounds might mean the same thing, or the same sound might mean two different things. It can depend on the circumstances."

"No wonder we have trouble understanding them," you say.

"But Jack," Dr. Vivaldi says, "you say the supercomputer deciphered some of it?"

Banta consults his notes for a moment. "This much was clear. Alceste was saying that it was time for him to go 'there.' Hermione said she understood."

"Go *there*," Dr. Vivaldi echoes. "But where?"

"That we don't know," Banta says. "The dolphins didn't need to say more. Hermione evidently knew what Alceste was referring to."

Turn to page 17.

You float where you are, trying to conserve energy. Although your life jacket keeps you afloat, you continue to move your arms and legs through the water to keep warm.

After about half an hour, you see a light moving across the sky, coming toward you. As it gets closer, you can see that it's a helicopter. You want to yell for help, but you know that the pilot could never hear you.

When the helicopter is almost directly over your head, a white flare suddenly lights up a round patch of sea, bright as day. Flashes of light reflect off the waves. You're right at the edge of the light, and you swim madly toward the center. Then, almost blinded as you look up at the flare, you jump half out of the water and frantically wave your arms.

The chopper roars overhead. The light is beginning to fade. You kick and splash and yell, trying to attract attention to yourself.

The helicopter circles, and another flare appears. Again you wave and splash. The helicopter swoops toward you. It hovers over your head. The wind from the rotors whips frothy tops on the waves.

Someone leans out of the hatch and drops a rope ladder. You swim toward the spot. You're saved!

Turn to page 73.

The chance of uncovering incredible riches is too great a temptation. A few days after the meeting a tidal wave strikes the island. There are no serious injuries, but Dr. Vivaldi announces that the institute will be closing for the rest of the summer in order to repair the property that was damaged. You pretend to leave the island with the other interns, but in actuality you take a room at a small inn nearby, using the extra money you brought along for the summer to pay your room and board. That weekend you go into town and walk along the docks where charter boats are lined up. One of them, named the *Emmy Lou,* has a sign that says "Cap'n Bob's Scuba Diving Trips." A man with a grizzled beard and a yachting cap is sitting on a deck chair on the dock, feet up on a crate, reading a magazine. You walk over to him.

Turn to page 51.

40

You can't pass up the chance to go windsurfing on such a perfect day. Frank Shaifer checks you, Dave, and Karen out on your sailboards. Dave has had quite a bit of experience, so he goes off on his own while Frank teaches you and Karen a few basic maneuvers. By the end of the day, you're sailing all over the cove. Twice, a couple of dolphins swim along with you.

For the rest of the week you and the other interns observe the dolphins' movements in the cove and make notes on their behavior. Each evening you type your notes into the computer.

Meanwhile, Dr. Vivaldi and Jack Banta try to follow a wandering dolphin in a blimp, hoping that it will lead them to a secret dolphin meeting place they've been theorizing about. Unfortunately, they lose track of it.

Turn to page 49.

A heated debate follows. Some people agree with Dr. Vivaldi, but others say it's wrong to withhold the news of such an important discovery. Finally Dr. Vivaldi agrees to put the matter to a vote. Opinion is so evenly balanced that it turns out that you have the deciding vote.

What will your vote be?

The End

You decide to play it safe and stay in the cove. You turn your board and race after Karen, trying to catch her. For the next hour or so, the two of you have a great time, sometimes racing each other, sometimes playing tag, and sometimes just sailing around. A couple of times you see a dolphin cruising along on the same track you're on. You wish a stronger wind would come up, so you could give the dolphin a good race.

But the wind stays about the same. That's why you're surprised when you hear a siren go off at the institute. The wailing sound carries all the way across the cove.

You glance over toward the dock. A flag with three red squares has gone up on the flagpole—the tsunami warning! A tidal wave is coming. You've got to get ashore and up on high ground fast.

Karen waves at you from her board—she's seen the warning and is heading for the dock. You glance out toward the inlet. There's no sign of Dave. He must be out in the ocean, out of earshot of the siren. You're worried about what will happen to him, but meanwhile you've got plenty to be scared about yourself.

Turn to page 106.

44

"Not build," Dr. Vivaldi says. "Find."

"How can that be?" Karen asks. "A city under the ocean?"

"It's like Atlantis," Dr. Vivaldi says. "This city might be called Pacifis. It was obviously built by some ancient island people of the Pacific. I would guess that the land it was built on slowly sank under the sea. For a while, the residents must have worked desperately to hold the water back with dikes. Then, perhaps, an earthquake struck, and the whole city was submerged. But it's remarkably well preserved."

"This is quite a discovery," you say.

"Indeed." Dr. Vivaldi runs her hand through her hair. Her mouth is drawn into a thin line.

"You seem worried, Nera," Banta says.

"I am," she replies. "The dolphins are so happy swimming around that city. They come from great distances to visit it. But if word got out about it, every treasure hunter in the world would be diving down there—looking for gold and jewels, littering the place, drilling, blasting, destroying the dolphins' world." She clenches her fists. "The dolphins have a secret, and we must keep it for them."

Go on to the next page.

As you listen to this, conflicting thoughts whirl through your mind. You'd like to let the dolphins keep their city untouched. But you can't help thinking about the unimaginable treasures that may be hidden there. You'd like to get in on the treasure hunt yourself. Obviously you can't do both.

If you decide to help keep the dolphin's city a secret, turn to page 90.

If you decide to become a treasure hunter, turn to page 39.

46

You look up at the sky, hoping that search planes might be out looking for you. What you see isn't encouraging—a line of heavy, dark clouds building in the north.

In the next hour the storm clouds pass by, and the sky clears. But your worries are far from over. There's still no sign of a search party. The sun climbs higher in the sky. You begin to get thirsty.

There is no shelter from the sun, but at least you can cool yourself in the foot or so of water under your feet. You and the others alternate standing, holding on to the radar mast, and sitting in the water, letting the gentle waves slosh over your legs and waist.

But you know that none of you will be able to keep this up for long without fresh water. By midafternoon, your throat is parched and your body weakened. You and your companions sit dazedly in the sea water. The thirst is tearing at your throats. You've got to get fresh water or you may not make it through the night.

Late in the afternoon, more trouble comes. The waves begin to grow steeper, sometimes rising as high as your neck. One wave strikes with such force that it jars the yacht partly off the reef.

You and the others stare at each other helplessly. You can tell by the looks in their eyes that they are thinking the same thing you are. There's not much time left.

Turn to page 103.

Then you spot a dolphin breaking the surface. You recognize the nick in the dorsal fin—it's Alceste! "I see him," you cry.

Dr. Vivaldi trains her binoculars on the spot where you're pointing, but the dolphin has already submerged. She watches until he surfaces again. "It's Alceste all right. Good work." She smiles at you. "Now comes the boring part I warned you about. You and I will take turns keeping Alceste in sight. I'll take the first shift. You might want to try to get some shut-eye—we don't know how far he's going, and we have to stay alert."

Turn to page 64.

The following Saturday is a free day, and you, Dave, and Karen decide to go windsurfing again.

"I'll be right here on the dock in case you run into any trouble out there," Frank says as the three of you are preparing to head out.

"Is it okay if we take our boards out through the inlet?" Dave asks. "I'd like to ride the rollers off the point."

Frank looks worried. "Too dangerous," he says, shaking his head.

"Dangerous? C'mon, man," Dave says. "It's the calmest day of the year out there. The ocean is like glass."

Frank shields his eyes while he looks out toward the point. "Well, it is unusually calm today. I guess it's okay, but stay within a hundred yards of the point. And if there's any change in sea conditions or the weather, come right in. Okay?"

Turn to page 71.

"Are you Cap'n Bob?" you ask.

"That's my handle," he says, barely looking up.

"Ever dive for treasure?"

He peers at you over the magazine. "Not in a long time. My customers mostly want to look at fish. We dive near reefs or old wrecks. The fish love wrecked ships."

"Would you be interested in looking for treasure?" you say.

The mariner takes off his cap and scratches his forehead. "Sure, if you know where some is."

"I do," you say.

He tosses the magazine aside and eyes you closely. "Really? How much treasure are you talking about?"

"A whole city full," you say.

"Oh, you don't say," he says. "Now who told you a yarn like that?" The captain's tone is sarcastic, but he has a glitter in his eye. You know he's interested, despite his skepticism.

"Let's just say I learned it from the dolphins," you say.

"You've been out at that Dolphin Institute?"

Turn to page 74.

52

The huge wave crashes onto the beach, sweeps over the dock and cabins, and rolls up the slope, carrying brush and debris, until it smacks against the main building. It washes back again. A smaller wave follows, then another only a few feet high.

The three of you start down from your perch. You're glad to be safe, but you're very worried about Dave and Frank.

You, Karen, and Pierre rush into the main lodge and radio the Coast Guard to report that two people are missing.

"We're swamped with calls—we'll search for them as soon as we can," the dispatcher says.

You lead the others down to the dock—or rather, where the dock used to be, because it has been carried away by the wave. The catamaran has broken loose from its mooring. It managed to ride the waves safely, but now the wind is blowing it toward the rocks. The institute's other boats have been washed up on the beach. Pierre grabs a dinghy.

"Help me pull this down to the water," he says. "We've got to get the catamaran."

At that moment Dr. Vivaldi's car pulls into the drive. She hops out, shouting to you. "I just came from Coast Guard headquarters. They found a skiff and a sailboard smashed on the coral reef!"

You all try to clean up some of the mess left by the tsunami as you wait anxiously for more news of Dave and Frank.

Turn to page 31.

Grace comes back to the cabin. "Nera, we're going to have to return to port. We're getting low on fuel."

"All right," Dr. Vivaldi says. "On the way, let's fly past that yacht. I want to get its registration number."

The blimp turns and flies past the yacht. You train your binoculars on the bow. A sheet of white sailcloth is hanging over the place where the registration number should be. You scan the deck and notice that someone is setting up a large piece of equipment. You watch curiously, wondering what it is.

"The echograph is showing up on display screen," Dr. Vivaldi cries excitedly. "It's hard to tell for sure, but it looks like the ruins of an ancient city!"

Turn to page 86.

You decide to follow Dave out through the inlet. You turn your board, and it picks up speed nicely. As you reach the inlet, however, you get stuck in the fierce chop where the incoming waves meet the outgoing tide.

Suddenly a nasty wave hits you, spilling you into the water. You hang on to your board, but you can't manage to right it in the rough water. You're drifting helplessly, and the current is taking you down the coast.

You hear a faint sound in the distance. It's the institute's warning siren, telling everyone to get ashore immediately. At first you think it must be a mistake. There's hardly a cloud in the sky. Then you realize what it must mean—a tsunami warning!

You try desperately to get up on your board, but the waves are too violent. All you can do is hang on. Only after you've drifted down the coast to calmer water are you able to stand again.

Turn to page 6.

56

You look out over the sparkling waters of the cove. "I hope I get a chance to do some sailing," you say eagerly. "I've never done it before."

"You sure will. Frank Shaifer's in charge of all the boats. He'll teach you everything you need to know. But I'll give you your first instruction right now. If you're ever out sailing and you see three red squares flying from the flagpole and hear a siren, come back in right away. It means there's a tsunami warning."

"Tsunami," you repeat. "You mean a tidal wave?"

"Right. We tend to have one every few years, and we're about due for one now. They occur anytime there's an earthquake under the Pacific."

"I hope I miss the next one," you say. "Are the other two interns here yet?"

"They are. They went into town with Dr. Vivaldi to get supplies. You'll meet all three of them at dinner."

You glance around. "So where are the dolphins? I thought they'd be in a big pool, but I don't see one."

Go on to the next page.

"Most people see dolphins in marine parks, so they expect that," Banta says. "But we believe you can't learn to communicate with dolphins by cooping them up in tanks, no matter how many fish you feed them. That's why we study the dolphins exclusively in their natural environment."

"Do you have a net at the entrance to the cove to keep them from escaping?"

The scientist shakes his head. "The dolphins are free to come and go. But they like it here. Some dolphins go away for months at a time, but they nearly always come back."

Turn to page 94.

58

You turn your board and race for the cove. The wind is behind you, and you make good time. Soon you're close enough to see the inlet. The water looks calmer now—you should have no trouble getting through.

You pass the point sailing at a good clip, but then you notice something strange happening. Your board is sliding back toward the ocean. A strong current has started running, as if all the water were emptying out of the cove!

You glance out to sea. In the distance a wall of water is rushing toward you—the tsunami. The water near the shore is running out to meet it.

No chance to get inside the cove now—you aim your board for the coral ledge along the nearest shore. You've got to beach your sailboard and get to high ground fast.

Try as you may, you can't make any progress. The current is pulling you back, sucking you into the huge wave. A minute later it breaks over you, smashing you and your board into pieces on the reefs.

The End

"Cap'n, let's get out of here," you say.

The skipper scowls. He doesn't move.

Harry steps toward him. "Let's put it this way," he says. "If you want to dive, you'll have to swim home."

Cap'n Bob cusses under his breath. "Okay, you've made your point." He throws the engines into gear and turns the wheel. The *Emmy Lou* heads south, toward land, and picks up speed.

You stand at the back of the boat looking through binoculars. A school of dolphins is churning up the water, leaping high out of the ocean and sending up huge sheets of water as they splash down. They almost seem to be dancing, as if they're happy you've left.

Turn to page 101.

The young dolphin's communication is followed by beeps from an older dolphin. This sound rises in pitch and volume. The computer translates it as "I am angry with you." Then there's nothing at all for a while, as if for some reason the dolphins decided to remain silent. Then another older dolphin says, "The fishing is good over here." After that comes more of the same kinds of simple things you heard on the first nine hours of the tapes.

You're disappointed not to have found more, but perhaps that one exchange can be deciphered. You play it for Karen when she returns, but she has no more idea than you do what it could be about.

A few hours later, Dr. Vivaldi and Dave return from their trip. Dr. Vivaldi is very excited.

"We found the place where the dolphins dive," she says. "While our blimp was hovering over it, a yacht passed nearby. Its captain radioed us. We didn't want to tip him off about the dolphins, so Dave told him that we were doing an oceanographic survey. The yacht went away, but we don't think we should send a diving party to the spot for a while. It could attract unwanted attention. There are a lot of people in the world who would be willing to destroy what the dolphins value down there if they thought there was treasure to be found."

She looks at you and Karen. "Did you find anything interesting listening to the computer tapes?"

Turn to page 110.

You've survived the tsunami, but your life is still in danger. Your sailboard is missing, probably smashed, and you're marooned on an inaccessible stretch of coast. The devastation along the shore must be terrible. You can't expect a quick rescue. You're probably just one of hundreds that are missing.

You slide down the muddy, matted bank to the shore. Your surfing shoes are no good on land, and the jungle is too thick to walk through anyway. You could try to swim for it, but you're exhausted from your ordeal, and the currents are tricky along this coast. Your chances of making it to the cove would be slim indeed.

As you're standing there trying to decide what to do, you notice a dolphin swimming very near to shore. It passes close to where you are, one eye fixed on you. It submerges, then quickly surfaces and heads toward you again.

You watch with amazement as the dolphin swims back and forth. You wonder if it could have been hit on the head by something and lost its sense of direction.

Then you get it—the dolphin must be trying to lead you along the shore.

Turn to page 8.

That night you're almost too excited to sleep. You can't wait to see what the summer holds in store.

Your biological clock hasn't yet adjusted to the change in time zones between the mainland and Hawaii. It's barely getting light the next morning when you sit up in bed, wide awake and ready to go. You head down to the dining room to see if you can get some breakfast. To your surprise, Banta is already there, sipping coffee and reading a scientific journal.

He looks up as you enter. "You're up early," he says with a smile. "The cook's not here yet, but there's plenty of milk and juice in the fridge, and you can help yourself to fresh pineapple, cereal, bananas, toast, whatever you want. While you're at it, put some bread in the toaster for me, will you?"

"Sure." You go to work in the kitchen. While you're waiting for the toast to pop, Banta comes in to pour himself some more coffee.

"What's scheduled for today?" you ask.

"Not much, actually, since it's Sunday. I'm going to spend most of the day in the lab, listening to tapes. I think I'm close to a discovery about what dolphins say to each other."

"That's cool. Can I come listen to the tapes?"

Turn to page 97.

64

During the hours that follow, you and Dr. Vivaldi take turns peering down at the traveling dolphin through your binoculars. Your patience pays off. About midafternoon of the second day, Alceste joins a large group of dolphins that are diving repeatedly in the same area, often staying down for fifteen or twenty minutes at a time.

"There's something down there that the dolphins find very interesting," you say. "What can it be?"

"I plan to find out," Dr. Vivaldi says. She begins to rig a hydrophone to a line. "We'll drop this into the water and see what we can hear. Then I'll drop a sonobuoy that will take echo pictures of the sea floor."

Grace keeps the blimp hovering about a hundred feet over the spot where the dolphins are diving. Dr. Vivaldi begins lowering the hydrophone into the water. You glance around, looking for more dolphins, and notice a small yacht about a mile away. It appears to be heading your way. You point it out to Dr. Vivaldi.

Turn to page 112.

You close your eyes and listen as carefully as you can. It's impossible to tell if any of the sounds means anything in particular, but one thing you notice is that the sounds on this tape seem much more complicated and varied than those on the first one. Once you even hear a sound like a flipper slapping the water, as if a dolphin might be gesturing to make a point. The thought makes you smile, though you know it's rather farfetched.

The tape ends. Banta cuts the scroll that has been printed out. Then he picks up the first scroll and pins the two tapes one above the other on the wall.

He turns to you. "You've heard the tapes. Here's how they look. Notice anything different about them?"

"The bottom one—the second recording— looks much more complicated," you say. "It has all sorts of extra squiggles and blips."

Banta nods. "No doubt about it. Whatever the dolphins were saying to each other, it's certain that they were communicating something much more complicated on the second recording than on the first."

"But how does that help us?"

Go on to the next page.

Banta apparently doesn't hear your question. He has returned to the computer and is busy punching in more commands. Without turning to look at you, he says, "I'm hooking this in to the supercomputer at the University of Hawaii. It's too sophisticated for our equipment to handle alone."

"Why do you think the second tape is so different from the first?" you ask.

Turn to page 13.

68

If you try to make it to shore, you're afraid you'll be in even greater danger when the wave strikes. You turn your board out toward the open sea, determined to be in deep water when the wave comes. Maybe then you can ride it out safely.

The current sweeps you along. You've covered about half a mile when you notice a bulge along the horizon ahead of you. In a few moments you see that it's a giant wall of water, heading straight for you—the tsunami!

Then you spot Dave, right in its path.

By now the current is carrying you fast—you couldn't escape if you wanted to. You stare with horror at what looks like a blue mountain rising above you.

The great wave reaches you, carrying you up as if on a high-speed escalator. The rippling water flings you off your board. You struggle in the water, still rising. But the wave doesn't break. In another moment you're sliding down the far side.

At last the water levels off. You look around, but Dave is nowhere in sight. Then you spot your board. The sail and mast have been swept away, but at least you have a life raft. You swim over and climb onto it. Then you turn and stare at the giant wave as it closes in on the shore.

Turn to page 117.

You immediately radio the yacht: "This is the blimp to the northwest. We are conducting a geographic survey. Please keep clear."

"Understood," someone on the yacht radios back. "We will comply with your request."

"Thank you." You sign off, then watch the yacht through your binoculars. It changes course, and after a moment you can see that there's a cloth draped over the registration numbers on the bow. When you tell Dr. Vivaldi this, she grabs the binoculars and takes a look.

"I'll notify the Coast Guard," she says. "Though the yacht will probably be gone by the time they can get out here to investigate."

When you get back to the Dolphin Institute, Dr. Vivaldi transmits her sonopictures to the supercomputer for analysis. She has the results by early the next day, and she calls together the staff members and interns to review them.

Banta, Karen, and Dave are eager to talk about what they've learned from studying tapes of dolphin conversations in the cove, but it's obvious that Dr. Vivaldi has more important news.

"The sound picture shows a whole city down there—the dolphins have a city!" she tells the assembled group, her voice betraying her excitement.

"You mean the dolphins can build cities?" Dave asks incredulously.

Turn to page 44.

"Sure thing," Dave says. He heads for the water, with his sailboard tucked under his arm. You and Karen follow.

Dave shoves off from the dock and makes straight for the entrance to the cove. He's headed out for the ocean, for sure.

"I'm staying in the cove," Karen calls to you. "Go on ahead if you want to."

It's been a calm day, but now there's a breeze springing up from the north—just enough so you can get up on your board and start sailing. You keep an eye out for dolphins, but none are surfacing nearby. It's like walking through the forest, you think. You know there are lots of animals around, but you can't see them.

You sail toward the inlet. It's rough there, where the rollers meet the wind-driven waves. If you spilled, you could have trouble righting yourself. The tide might carry you out to sea, or the wind might shift so that you couldn't get back against it. Frank can't see the inlet from the dock, so he'd have no way of knowing if you were in trouble. And you aren't as experienced at this as Dave is.

Still, it looks like a lot of fun out there. Dave waves and gestures for you to follow him.

*If you stay in the cove,
turn to page 43.*

*If you sail through the inlet,
turn to page 54.*

The helicopter pilot takes you to the Coast Guard base. Jack Banta is there to greet you, along with a doctor and several FBI agents. After you shower and change into dry clothes, Banta hands you a sandwich and leads you into an office, where the agents and some Coast Guard officers are waiting. You tell them the whole story while you're eating.

Within two hours Coast Guard search planes locate the yacht you described, just as it's heading into Pearl Harbor. By the time it docks, the police and the FBI are waiting. Dr. Vivaldi and Grace Segovia are rescued, and the criminals are apprehended—all thanks to you!

Turn to page 95.

"I was a summer intern, but not anymore," you answer. "There are better things to do."

"Okay," Cap'n Bob says, getting to his feet. "Just where is this city full of treasure? Can you find it on a chart?"

"Yes," you say. "I know the latitude and longitude. I'll show you once we're on our way. You can bring anyone else along that you want. But I get half of anything we find. You get the other half. You can split it up any way you want."

Cap'n Bob looks you in the eye. "You're a tough bargainer," he says. "How far away is this treasure?"

"About a hundred and fifty miles," you say. "We can get there in a day, if the weather stays this good."

He looks up at the deep blue sky. "Weather looks like it will hold," he says. "But how can I be sure you know what you're talking about?"

"Look," you say, "I wouldn't want to spend a couple of days rocking around in a small boat if I didn't have a good reason."

The mariner chews on his lip for a moment. Then he says, "Business is kind of slow right now. Guess I'll take a chance. Not much to lose."

Go on to the next page.

"And a lot to gain," you say.

He scowls at you. "Yeah—I've heard that one before."

The following morning at 6:00 A.M. you board the *Emmy Lou*. Cap'n Bob and his first mate, Harry, are already on deck.

Turn to page 22.

"I'll go with you on the blimp," you say.

"Good." Dr. Vivaldi is already headed toward the door. "Get your things together," she says over her shoulder. "Hurry."

A few minutes later you and Dr. Vivaldi are in her car on your way to the airport. You hang on to the handgrip as Dr. Vivaldi whips the car around one mountainous curve after another. You reach the airport in what must be record time, and screech to a stop in front of the blimp.

A short, dark-haired woman wearing a tan flight jacket breaks off her conversation with two ground personnel and walks briskly toward you.

"So, Nera," she calls to Dr. Vivaldi. "Here I am, ready to go dolphin chasing."

Dr. Vivaldi jumps out of the car. "You're great to do this on such short notice, Grace."

"What can I say. I like excitement," Grace says with a grin.

Dr. Vivaldi turns and introduces you.

Grace gives you a vigorous handshake, then turns back to Dr. Vivaldi. "Frank Shaifer called a couple of minutes ago. He said that when he lost sight of Alceste, the dolphin was swimming at about ten knots, heading north-northwest."

"Then there's no time to lose," Dr. Vivaldi says. "Let's get going."

Turn to page 23.

A few feet from shore, the dolphin turns, and you slide off into the ankle-high water. You wish there were a way to thank her. But when you turn around, all you see is her tail, loudly slapping the water before she submerges.

Karen comes running toward you. "You're safe!" she calls. "It's a miracle!"

"I guess it is," you say as you wade out of the water. You're happy to be in one piece. More than that, you're thrilled by what happened to you. You can't wait to tell Dr. Vivaldi what you've just learned about dolphins!

The End

Fifteen minutes later, you're all safely aboard the chopper, headed back to shore. Sitting in the cabin, sipping cold, fresh water, you take turns telling the Coast Guard officers what happened. They immediately radio a report in to the command station.

The Coast Guard has no trouble finding the lifeboat with Mr. X and his cohorts in it. It turns out that they're already wanted for other crimes, and the Coast Guard and the police award you and your friends with special medals in honor of your part in their capture.

This makes you feel good, but something else happens that makes you feel even better. Everyone who learned about the city of the dolphins agrees to keep the information a secret. With luck, the dolphins will be able to enjoy their playground for hundreds of years, undisturbed by human interference.

The End

80

The *Emmy Lou* ploughs through a light chop on the ocean most of the day. It's about four in the afternoon when Cap'n Bob yells down from the wheelhouse, "Latitude north twenty-two degrees fifty feet; longitude west one hundred fifty-eight degrees seventeen feet. That's where you told us to go, and that's where we are. Does it look familiar?"

Harry guffaws, and you smile a little at this joke. One patch of ocean looks like any other.

"Depth here is only ninety feet, and very irregular," Cap'n Bob says. "We could be over that city of yours right now."

"Hey, a dolphin!" Harry shouts suddenly.

You and Cap'n Bob turn to look where he's pointing. One dolphin after another arches out of the water, their eyes on your boat. After a moment they dive and disappear beneath the waves.

"I have the feeling this is the spot," you say.

"Okay." Bob throttles down to idling speed. "Get your scuba gear on. We can get a dive in before sunset."

Harry, who is an expert diver, helps you with your scuba gear, shows you how it works, and reviews the safety rules with you. Meanwhile, Cap'n Bob has rigged up a ladder and a floating platform at the stern of the boat. You and Harry step onto the platform and leap into the ocean.

Turn to page 102.

The water is up to your chin by the time you reach the ladder, but you manage to scramble up to the main cabin. Then you glance back down. Another minute or so and you probably would have drowned.

The yacht is sinking fast now. You follow Dr. Vivaldi and Grace through the main cabin and up another ladder to the top deck, where you look around for the remaining lifeboat. But Mr. X and his two henchmen are already in it, motoring away from the sinking ship.

By now the water is sloshing around your feet even here on the top deck. Dr. Vivaldi scrambles up to the roof over the control station—the highest point on the yacht. You and Grace follow. The three of you perch there, gripping the radar mast.

"About half a minute till we're in the drink," Dr. Vivaldi says. "Didn't even have time to get life vests."

At that moment you feel a jolt. The yacht lurches and then stabilizes.

"We're aground," you exclaim. "It's not going to sink any more."

Dr. Vivaldi lets out a sigh of relief.

Grace peers over the side. "We'll be safe for a while, unless the weather turns bad on us."

Dr. Vivaldi scans the horizon, shading her eyes with one hand. "It looks good now, but the seas don't stay this calm for long around here."

Turn to page 46.

Then the dolphins are gone, and Cap'n Bob is yelling to you from the boat. "That was incredible! You two okay?"

Harry must be. He's laughing so hard he gets water down his windpipe. He starts coughing and wheezing and barely makes it to the boat. Cap'n Bob helps him aboard, then gives you a hand up over the rail.

"There are ruins of a city down there," you say as you step aboard. "It's amazing." You sit on the deck, rubbing your chest. Your rib cage is a little sore from having been pushed so hard by the dolphin.

Cap'n Bob slaps his knee. "We've got it made," he cries. "A whole city down there, with plenty of treasure, I bet, and nothing but dolphins to guard it."

"Why would dolphins guard treasure?" you ask. "Gold and jewels aren't worth anything to them."

"Just the same," Cap'n Bob says, "I'm sure there's something valuable down there. And I'm going to find out what it is."

"I don't want to go down there again," Harry says. "The dolphins might get rougher next time."

"I'll dive down there myself and take my spear gun," Cap'n Bob says. "I think the dolphins will be smart enough to stay clear of me."

Turn to page 116.

In the years ahead, whenever you're at the ocean, you always look out, hoping to see dolphins playing among the waves, and you think about what Dr. Vivaldi said about their different world. As much as you respect the scientist, you're not sure you agree with her. Someday you hope to return to Hawaii and get to know the dolphins better. You'd like dolphins and people not just to be at peace with each other but to be friends.

The End

"How can we do that?" you ask.

"Simple," Dr. Vivaldi says. "We have to record the dolphins in a place where they can't possibly expect it. Then if our theory is correct, we'll hear more of the kind of speech made by the young dolphin on this tape."

"So all we have to do is figure out how to listen in on them without their knowing it," Dave says.

"Easier said than done," Dr. Vivaldi replies. "They know all our boats. They probably watch everything we do. They know our moves much better than we know theirs."

"I know," you say. "Have one of the local fishermen put down a microphone hidden by bait. Like that man who goes out in his dory every morning. He likes to fish outside the inlet, where the tide is coming by the point. The dolphins would never suspect him."

"Good idea," Dr. Vivaldi says. "I know the fisherman you mean—his name is Nikko, and he lives in that shack at the end of the cove. The institute is one of his best customers. I'm sure he'll let you go out with him. He's got a small cabin on the boat. You'll have to stay in it most of the time so the dolphins can't see you, but from there you can make a recording of what the microphone picks up."

"I have a feeling this is going to be our breakthrough," you say. "I can't wait to hear what I get on that tape."

Turn to page 28.

At that moment you realize the equipment being set up on the yacht is a missile launcher—and it's aimed right at you!

"Grace, get us out of here, quickly!" you shout. "These people are dangerous!"

Suddenly there's an explosion. The blimp lurches, tilts sharply, and starts to fall.

Grace is yelling into the radio. "Mayday! Mayday!" She turns to you. "Sit down and hold on tight. We're going down!"

You and Dr. Vivaldi strap yourselves in your seats and bend over to brace yourselves. The blimp drops abruptly, twists, and then rises for a few seconds, careening like a balloon losing air. Then it falls steadily.

THUNK. The gondola slaps down on the water. It quickly sinks below the surface, then bobs up again. The door has been ripped off, and water starts pouring in.

Turn to page 34.

You're awakened at dawn by a terrible crunching, grinding sound. The yacht lurches, tilting to one side.

Dr. Vivaldi and Grace rush over and peer out the porthole.

"We're aground," the scientist says. "Hung up on a reef!"

"Must be Lakai Reef," Grace says. "That's the only thing close by, but how—?" Her voice trails off, and she shakes her head, looking confused.

Suddenly the answer is clear to you. "The dolphins towed us," you exclaim. "I heard them last night. They must have chewed through the anchor line."

"Incredible," Dr. Vivaldi cries. "That must be it—there's no other logical explanation. This is wonderful news for our research."

"It may not be so wonderful for us, though," Grace says. "Look." She points to the lower side of the deck. Water is gushing in through cracks in the floorboards.

"We'll be flooded. We've got to get out of here," you say.

Go on to the next page.

You, Grace, and Dr. Vivaldi throw your weight against the wooden door. The wood cracks, but it doesn't give way. Finally, after a few more tries, you feel the door give and open a little. More water rushes in. It's knee-deep and rising rapidly. You force the door far enough open to squeeze through.

The three of you wade down the passageway. The electricity has gone off, and you have only the shaft of daylight coming down the companionway ahead of you to guide your way.

Turn to page 82.

You all agree to keep your discovery a secret so that the dolphins will never be disturbed in their city.

About a week later a tsunami, a tidal wave caused by an underwater earthquake, strikes the north coast of Kauai, carrying away the institute's boats, dock, and shorefront cabins. Fortunately there is ample warning and no one is injured, but your stay at Luali Cove will be cut short. Dr. Vivaldi announces that the institute will have to close for repairs.

At dinner the night before you and the other interns are to leave, Dr. Vivaldi holds another staff meeting.

"I was hoping for something other than a tidal wave this summer," she says. "I'd feel better if we had learned to communicate with the dolphins as we hoped. Perhaps I'm wrong, but I have a feeling that the dolphins could speak to us but have chosen not to. We are scientists who want to learn everything we can about nature. But we also want to respect nature and respect intelligent creatures just as we would other humans. Therefore, I've decided that I'm not going to investigate dolphins any further. As far as I'm concerned, they have their world and we have ours. And I'm not sure which is better."

Turn to page 84.

You dive under the air bag and come up in a bubble about three feet across. That should give you enough air for at least an hour, and your life jacket makes it easy to stay afloat.

You hear the yacht approaching. Its propellers reverse, bringing it to a stop. Over the sound of the idling engines you hear a winch cranking, then a splash. You figure the people on the yacht must have lowered a boat and taken Dr. Vivaldi and Grace on board.

Then you hear the engines revving up again. The yacht circles around the air bag. Suddenly there's the sound of machine gun fire!

Bullets rip through the air bag, some of them missing you by inches. After a few seconds the barrage stops, and the sound of the yacht's engine fades rapidly, as if it's speeding away.

You stay under the bubble for about ten more minutes, then dive under the air bag and swim hard.

Turn to page 32.

"Let's go for it, Cap'n," you say with a grin. "I don't want to throw away the chance of finding some of that valuable treasure you were just talking about."

"Good." Cap'n Bob turns and starts putting on his scuba gear.

Harry slumps in his seat. He keeps shaking his head, saying, "I don't like it, I don't like it."

Cap'n Bob pokes you in the ribs, forgetting they're sore. "Harry's a superstitious sort," he says. "I've never been able to teach him to get over it." He picks up his spear gun. "I'll go down and check things out while you rest up from your last dive, kid. Then, if all goes well, we'll go down together." He gives a mock salute and goes over the side, spear gun in hand.

You and Harry stand at the rail, looking anxiously down at the water, waiting for Cap'n Bob to come up.

A half hour passes. You know his air must be running out. "One of us should go down after him," you say to Harry.

Harry shakes his head. "That would be foolish. There's nothing we can do to help him now."

You nod silently, knowing that Harry is right. Cap'n Bob will never be seen again.

You and Harry turn the *Emmy Lou* back toward Kauai. The two of you agree never to tell anyone about the city of the dolphins. As far as you know, it's still there.

The End

"There are some now," you exclaim. You've just spotted the graceful, arched backs of two dolphins, surfacing and then diving as they swim past the dock.

Banta shields his eyes and looks out over the water. "Alceste and Hermione—I can tell by their markings. Alceste has a nick in his dorsal fin. They probably know a new intern has arrived and have decided to investigate."

"You're kidding."

Banta raises one eyebrow. "I think I'm kidding," he says, "but . . . who knows?"

Turn to page 25.

The next day Dr. Vivaldi calls together everyone at the institute for a meeting. "We've made a remarkable discovery," she says, once you're all seated around the big table in the dining room. "The dolphins have a special place in the ocean where they like to meet and play. This in itself is quite fascinating, but the echograph I saw moments before the blimp went down indicated that the dolphins' playground might be the ruins of an ancient city. We must investigate further, but I'd rather not mention it to the press. I think we should keep it to ourselves."

"But why?" Banta says. "That kind of publicity might help us get more funding for our programs."

"That's true," she agrees. "But it would also encourage treasure seekers to come in droves. That place belongs to the dolphins, and I don't want to be the cause of its conquest by humans."

Turn to page 41.

You start swimming. But darkness comes on fast, and soon you can't even see your hand in front of your face, let alone the dolphins. You swim on, hoping that you're still heading in the right direction.

You've been swimming for about half an hour when you hear the noise of an approaching engine. You stop swimming and turn around just as a brilliant flare bursts over the water. Silhouetted in its light is a rescue helicopter, flying in tight circles over the spot where the blimp went down. If only you were still there!

You take a few strokes toward the helicopter, then slow as the light from the flare fades. You're sure that the helicopter will never keep hovering long enough for you to make it back there.

Another flare lights up near the first one. You start swimming again a little faster, but you're almost exhausted as you plow halfheartedly toward the light.

The second flare fades, and the helicopter veers away. Suddenly it's coming toward you, fast! You look up hopefully, but no other flares drop. The chopper roars over your head and in a few moments is out of sight.

Turn to page 14.

The scientist takes a sip of his coffee. "You're welcome to join me, though I'm afraid you might get pretty bored, sitting around listening to whistles and clicks. It's going to be a beautiful day—I heard the other interns talking about trying out the sailboards. Frank Shaifer is a real pro at windsurfing. I know he'd be glad to give you some lessons."

You glance out at the cove, shimmering in the early morning light. Windsurfing sounds like a lot of fun. On the other hand, Banta said he might be on the verge of a new discovery. It would be awfully exciting to be a part of it.

*If you decide to go windsurfing,
turn to page 40.*

*If you decide to join Banta in the lab,
turn to page 114.*

You decide to take your chances with the people on the yacht. In a few minutes you, Grace, and Dr. Vivaldi are being roughly pulled aboard. The men who seize you lock you in a forward stateroom. Soon afterward, the door opens. A fat man in a white suit strides in. He motions you back against the far wall. Another man, brandishing a submachine gun, stands behind him, his finger on the trigger.

"So," the fat man says, "you are Dr. Vivaldi, and this is one of your interns."

"You seem to know all about us," Dr. Vivaldi says. "And who are you?"

"You may call me Mr. X," the fat man says, "and all you need to know about me is that I am a scientist, just like you."

"Scientists don't kidnap their colleagues," Dr. Vivaldi says sharply.

"Silence." Mr. X reddens with anger. "You will not speak except to answer my questions! Understood?"

Dr. Vivaldi remains silent.

"Good. Then we can begin. First, we know you have some interesting information about the dolphins. Have you told anyone about how they congregate around this spot?"

The moment you hear this you suspect a trap. You're about to answer that other scientists have been informed when Dr. Vivaldi says, "No, it's important that this information remain secret."

Turn to page 7.

"Fair enough," Banta says. "On that basis we'll keep up the secret monitoring of the dolphin talk for now. But what I'd really like to do is follow Alceste on his trip *there.*"

"If he hasn't already left," you say.

"He may have. I saw him off the dock just before breakfast," Frank says. "He nudged against some other dolphins and then took off toward the inlet."

"We could follow him in the catamaran," you say.

Frank shakes his head. "Alceste would know that we were following him."

Dr. Vivaldi nods. "Dolphins can hear boats miles away, even sailboats. If this place is something they talk about only in secret, they're certainly not going to lead us to it."

"If only there were another way of following him," Banta says.

Dr. Vivaldi looks thoughtful for a moment. Suddenly she grins. "There *is* another way. You've all seen that advertising blimp over the island. Grace Segovia, the owner, is a good friend of mine. She's fascinated by dolphins—in fact she's one of the trustees of the institute. We could follow Alceste in the blimp."

Banta's face lights up. "It's perfect! Dolphins aren't afraid of birds or planes. They don't care if it's going to rain. They aren't in the habit of looking up at the sky."

Turn to page 21.

The next day, back on Kauai, you book the next plane to the mainland. When you get home, you read every magazine and newspaper article about dolphins you can get your hands on. Only one article catches your eye. It tells of a yacht named the *Sea Fox* that mysteriously sank in fair weather about ninety miles north of the island of Kauai. The men who were on it—most of whom had criminal records—were found days later, drifting in their life raft. They seemed frightened out of their wits and wouldn't tell anyone what had happened, but they all swore they'd never go near the spot again.

You can't help smiling when you read this. You're sure the men who were rescued were trying to take treasure from the dolphins. The animals must have taught them a quite a lesson.

You whistle a tune and walk with a light step for the rest of the day. You have a feeling that no one will disturb the dolphins again. You'll always be able to think of them chasing fish, calling to each other, playing among the ruins, and living free from care in their underwater city.

The End

102

You descend slowly through silvery-blue layers of ocean, straining to see what's on the bottom. The first thing you see is a submerged coral reef running along the ocean floor, like the backbone of a mountain ridge. Strange and beautiful plants and coral formations protrude from the reef. Hundreds of colorful species of fish swim about.

Then you see an astonishing sight—the ruins of an underwater stone building, its roof missing, its columns broken or fallen. There's a smaller building beside it, mostly intact, and nearby is a row of columns with arched spans supporting what's left of a marble roof. You've found the underwater city, the playground of the dolphins!

You look off to one side and almost faint with fear. A shark is coming at you! A second later you realize it's not a shark, but a dolphin.

But why is it coming so close? Maybe it wants you to pet it. You hold out your arms. The dolphin nuzzles into your stomach, causing you to bend forward. You wrap your arms around its snout, trying to reduce the pressure on your stomach. The dolphin is not hurting you, but it keeps moving, propelling you upward ever more steeply until you break through the surface, still perched on its nose. With a final thrust the dolphin tosses you high in the air. You come down with a tremendous splash. A second later another dolphin sends Harry even higher in the air, and he too lands with a splash.

Turn to page 83.

Another hour passes. The sun is low on the horizon now, and a chilly breeze from the north is stirring up the sea. You cling to the radar mast as one wave after another crashes over you.

Most of the day you felt too hot—now you feel too cold. That doesn't make you any less thirsty, however. Your need for water is desperate.

"Look!" Dr. Vivaldi is pointing to the south. A helicopter is heading toward a point about half a mile to the east. The chopper is close enough so you can see the two orange Coast Guard stripes on the side. You jump and wave wildly. Dr. Vivaldi takes off her faded red polo shirt and swings it in great loops over her head. Then a wave hits her, and she has to fight to stay on the platform. But the helicopter is turning. The pilot has seen you!

Turn to page 79.

104

You're barely listening—you're too amazed by the strange sight unfolding in front of you. The cove is now almost half empty, and it's still draining! Tremendous rapids have formed at the inlet. You know that very soon all that water will be coming back—and a lot more.

Then you see the wave—a monstrous mountain of water pouring through the inlet, sweeping over the coral ridges along the shore. The sound is like thunder that doesn't end.

You stare at the wave, holding your breath, wondering whether you'll all be swept away. But to your great relief you see that the wave is flattening out as it spreads across the cove. By the time it reaches shore it's only about fifteen feet high.

Turn to page 52.

You turn and set your course straight for the dock. Frank Shaifer is standing on the edge, motioning wildly to you to hurry up. He jumps in the skiff, starts the outboard, and casts off. A moment later he's under way, headed for the inlet. You know he's going after Dave. You just hope they both get back safely.

Dr. Vivaldi has gone into town for the day, and Jack Banta is visiting a friend on the other side of the island. The only adult left at the institute besides Frank Shaifer is the manager and chef, Pierre Ravel. Karen reaches the dock first, and Pierre helps her get her board safely stowed in the equipment shed. You come in a moment later.

"When's it expected to hit?" you ask breathlessly.

"Sometime within the next hour, that's all I know," he says. "They say it's just a small earth tremor off the coast but that the wave may be fifteen feet high, maybe higher."

Fortunately, the main lodge is set at least twenty feet above sea level. Still, as a precaution, you, Karen, and Pierre scramble up the bluff behind the lodge. Here, more than thirty feet above the sea, you should be safe from almost anything.

Go on to the next page.

The three of you wait there, watching for the water level in the cove to drop. Pierre has told you how that will be the sign the tidal wave is coming.

None of you says much. You're too worried thinking about Dave and Frank out there on the ocean.

"Look at the end of the dock," Pierre suddenly says.

Turn to page 26.

108

You decide to stay in the lab at the cove after all. Both Karen and Dave eagerly volunteer to go along on the blimp. Dr. Vivaldi flips a coin, and Dave wins. A matter of minutes later, the two of them leave for the airfield.

All day you and Karen pore over tapes of dolphin talk picked up by the secret microphone Banta has hidden in a coral reef. Banta stays long enough to help you get started, then leaves to run some errands in town. For hours you listen as the dolphins chatter away. With the computers programmed to pick up speech patterns, you can understand a good deal. For example: "Good fishing this way"; "Come play with me"; "Small sharks in cove—keep babies guarded."

Understanding these simple speech patterns is a huge advance over previous attempts to decipher dolphin communication. But scientists have suspected that dolphins communicate in simple ways for a long time. There is nothing in all the hours of tapes so far to suggest that dolphins are as smart as people. In fact, the communications that the scientists at the institute have been deciphering are hardly more complicated than might be found in a family of elephants or a troop of chimpanzees.

Go on to the next page.

The recorder was set to tape twelve hours of continuous dolphin talk. After listening to about seven hours' worth of tape, Karen goes out for a walk to stretch her legs. But you've resolved to listen to all twelve hours. Hearing patterns repeated again and again is the only way you can begin to understand what the dolphins are saying.

The only unusual thing that you hear on the tapes is a series of high-pitched clicks that occurs after about nine hours. The computer reports, "Source: a very young dolphin; sounds not recorded before; meaning unknown."

Turn to page 61.

110

You describe the odd exchange you heard and play it for Dr. Vivaldi and Dave. "Do you have any idea what was being communicated?" you ask. "The computer is stumped."

Dr. Vivaldi shakes her head. "Let's see if we can figure this out. The young dolphin said something that caused an older dolphin to get angry. We don't know what the young one said —there's no past record of it, and the surrounding circumstances don't give a clue."

"So it's useless for the moment?" Dave says.

"Not at all. It tells us something astonishing. We've never heard a dolphin respond angrily in quite this tone. In my opinion the young dolphin said something that offended the older one."

Suddenly you have an idea. "Or maybe the young dolphin said something the older ones didn't want humans to hear." You recall what Banta told you about the dolphins saying certain kinds of things among themselves when they were sure humans were not listening.

"So you're proposing that the dolphins may have a secret language they don't use around humans—perhaps one much more complicated than what we hear," Dr. Vivaldi says thoughtfully. "It sounds possible, I suppose. Of course, this is just a theory. As scientists, we must test it out."

Turn to page 85.

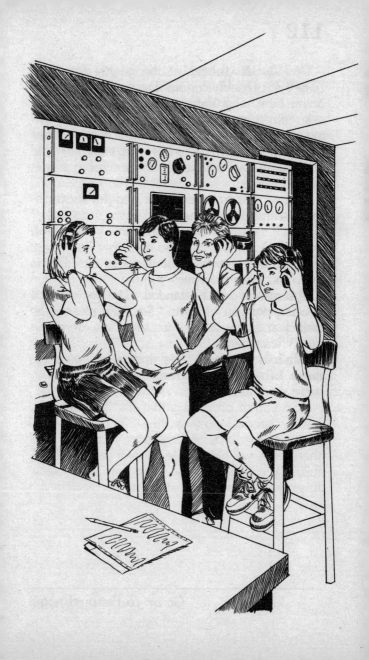

112

Dr. Vivaldi glances at the yacht, scowling. "They're probably curious about what a blimp is doing here. Call them on the radiophone and ask them to stay well clear. Tell them we're doing scientific research." Dr. Vivaldi straps on her earphones and hunches over the small portable computer that will help her monitor the dolphins' sounds.

You set the transmitter for general short-distance transmission, then hold down the speaker button. "Yacht on course 045, this is the blimp dead ahead of you, do you read me?"

The answer comes back immediately. "This is *Sea Fox*. We read you."

You glance out the window. The yacht is still heading right toward you. *"Sea Fox,* please stay well clear of this area," you say. "We are doing scientific research."

"This is *Sea Fox*. We understand your request. What kind of scientific research?"

Go on to the next page.

You're not sure how to respond. You remember Banta's warning about all the unscrupulous people who would like to use the dolphins for their own greedy purposes. Maybe you should pretend to be conducting a geographic survey or something, just in case. But the voice from the *Sea Fox* sounded friendly and curious, not threatening. Besides, the yacht is probably close enough by now for its passengers to see the dolphins themselves. If they suspect that you're lying, it could pique their curiosity even more—and if they don't change course soon, the whole project will be ruined.

If you tell the truth, turn to page 30.

If you tell them you're conducting a geographic survey, turn to page 70.

114

You decide to spend the day with Banta. He leads you to his lab, a soundproof room at the back of the lodge. He points out various pieces of special equipment. "You'll be hearing the sounds of our dolphins on that speaker. They're from a recording I made just yesterday. The sound waves will be displayed graphically on that video screen. This machine over here prints the readout on a long roll of paper. The lines look squiggly and meaningless, but we can often find patterns in them that we wouldn't notice just listening to the tapes." Banta flips a switch. "Listen to this."

A moment later you hear a dolphin call— *wrrrupp, wrrrupp, wrrrupp,* then a series of clicks, then a sound like a warbling bird.

The sounds are pretty and interesting, but you don't know how anyone could figure out what they mean. Banta looks quite excited, however.

"Can you tell what the dolphins are saying?" you ask.

"I have a few ideas," he says. "But I have to run this acoustical data through the computer. It's programmed to identify patterns of sound and suggest ways they might relate to each other."

Turn to page 12.

116

Harry stands up and looks over the side. There are several dolphins cruising along on the surface about a hundred feet away. He turns back to Cap'n Bob. "Listen, Skipper, I think we'd better get out of here. I got bad feelings about what's going to happen if we stay around."

Cap'n Bob looks over at you. "What do you think? You're the one who got us out here. Are you with me or not?"

If you decide to dive again with Cap'n Bob, turn to page 93.

If you advise Cap'n Bob to take the hint and leave, turn to page 60.

Three hours later, you're rescued by a Coast Guard helicopter. You help the pilot look for Dave, and a few minutes later you spot him, clinging to the remains of his board.

When the two of you get back to the institute, you find that the dock and some of the boats were destroyed by the tsunami and that the main building was damaged. Fortunately, everyone got to high ground in time to escape injury. However, Dr. Vivaldi announces that the institute will have to close for repairs for the rest of the summer. In a few days, you and the other interns will be heading home.

The night before you leave, you dream you are a dolphin, riding a tsunami high over the ocean, surfing endlessly on its crest. It's the most wonderful dream you've ever had.

The End

ABOUT THE AUTHOR

EDWARD PACKARD is a graduate of Princeton University and Columbia Law School. He developed the unique storytelling approach used in the Choose Your Own Adventure series while thinking up stories for his children Caroline, Andrea, and Wells.

ABOUT THE ILLUSTRATOR

TOM LA PADULA graduated from Parsons School of Design with a BFA and earned his MFA from Syracuse University.

For over a decade Tom has illustrated for national and international magazines, advertising agencies, and publishing houses. Besides his illustrating, Tom is on the faculty of Pratt Institute, where he teaches a class in illustration.

During the spring of 1992, his work was exhibited in the group show "The Art of the Baseball Card" at the Baseball Hall of Fame in Cooperstown, New York. In addition, the corporation Johnson & Johnson recently acquired one of Tom's illustrations for their private collection.

Mr. La Padula has illustrated *The Luckiest Day of Your Life, Secret of the Dolphins, Scene of the Crime,* and *The Secret of Mystery Hill* in the Choose Your Own Adventure series. he resides in New Rochelle, New York, with his wife, son, and daughter.

CHOOSE YOUR OWN ADVENTURE®